CHEE-LIN

〜

A GIRAFFE'S JOURNEY

by James Rumford

HOUGHTON MIFFLIN COMPANY   BOSTON 2008

for Sally Santucci Goetz

The Tribute Giraffe with Attendant
by Shen Du (1357–1434)
PHILADELPHIA MUSEUM OF ART:
Gift of John T. Dorrance, 1977

麒

chee [qí]

麟

lin [lín]

Eighty years before Columbus set sail in 1492, China sent a fleet of ships to explore the world. The Chinese discovered many marvelous things, but of these discoveries, one stands out as the most marvelous of all: the *chee-lin*.

In Chinese mythology, the chee-lin was a horned beast with the body of a deer, the tail of an ox, and the hooves of a horse. Whenever the emperor was good and wise and the people content, there appeared a chee-lin. Only once in China's long history had a chee-lin appeared. That was at the birth of their wise man, Confucius.

But two thousand years later, in our fifteenth century, another chee-lin appeared . . . this time out of Africa. This chee-lin was just a giraffe, but to the Chinese, it was an omen of good fortune.

The Smell of Rain

In the fine rain of East Africa, Tweega, a newborn giraffe, struggled to stand.

He raised his long neck and breathed in the wet smell of the land. Slowly he rose, wobbling. Up he went until he towered and teetered six feet above the grass.

His mother, twice as tall, nudged him gently to her milk. As he drank, the rain danced on his glistening coat without making a sound.

In the Blink of an Eye

BY THE END OF THE FIRST MONTH, Tweega began to eat on his own. He tried the leaves of the whistling thornbush, but stinging ants hiding in its branches got him every time. So he stayed close to his mother for her milk and her protection, watching her every move.

There was danger, but Tweega did not fear it. There were lions, but his mother had powerful legs that could kick. There were men, but the tallest giraffes could spot their shining skin a mile away and carry the herd off to safety. That is when Tweega would run, and with his short neck, he was faster than his mother, faster than the tall, lumbering bulls.

At four months, Tweega had grown to eight feet. He strode through the grass with red-billed oxpeckers perched on his neck. As he nibbled on his favorite leaves, the oxpeckers searched for insects in his fur. Everything was as it should be.

Full from eating, Tweega dozed—with his eyes wide open, for never once did he lose sight of his mother, who was just a bush or two away. But it happened that on one particular day, when his mother disappeared behind a tall acacia, Tweega closed his eyes to the sun's glare. That's all it took: a second.

Up from the grass, like striking snakes, came ropes and lassos. They circled his neck and bound his legs. Tweega's mouth opened with surprise. His eyes darkened with anger. His stomach tightened with fear.

He had been captured!

The Prize

At that moment, the red-billed birds scattered, calling out an alarm to the rest of the herd. Tweega's mother came running, but the shining men shouted and raised their spears. Bleating, Tweega lifted his head from the ground and saw his frightened mother flee with the rest of the herd to safety.

The shining men laughed and whooped.

"Such a fine animal!" they said.

"A real beauty!" they shouted.

"A prize for the sultan!"

The men hobbled Tweega's legs just enough so that he could walk but could not kick. The ropes around his neck stopped him from butting them with his head. In this way, the men took Tweega from his homeland.

That night the smell of the campfire filled his nostrils. Surely the flames would soon be upon him. Tweega strained at his ropes until he gave up. Trembling in the starry night, he waited for the end.

On the Beach

BUT DAWN CAME and many days after that as the men slowly led Tweega to the African coast. The grassland changed to jungle. The air grew thick with moist heat. It smelled of flowers and people, crowds of them chattering and running about. Tweega had arrived at the town of Malindi.

In Malindi, Tweega's captors sold him to the sultan, who lived by the sea.

That afternoon, tied up in the sultan's compound, Tweega looked out on the endless Indian Ocean and saw waves for the first time. The waves sparkled and danced like wet-season grass in the breeze. Tweega took the ocean's salty breath into his lungs. He grew quiet and stopped pulling at his ropes.

Then a tall boy, who was part of the sultan's household, brought buckets of water and washed Tweega. What a relief! It had been days since Tweega had felt the red-billed birds on his back. And without a tree to scratch against or his mother to rub against, he was crawling with ticks.

Tall-Boy did not shout like the others but whispered. And as he brushed Tweega, Tweega closed his eyes in peace.

Every day Tall-Boy brought Tweega leaves from the thorn tree and cool, clear water. He even sang to him in the evening light.

توقِ الزراف

After a time, Tall-Boy took the ropes off Tweega, except for the one round his neck.

"Best to stay here so that I can care for you," he whispered to Tweega one day. "Besides, you have nowhere to go."

But Tall-Boy couldn't have been more wrong.

Sailing Before the Monsoon

At that moment, men were loading up their dhows with goods. They worked fast, hoping to catch the first winds of the season to Arabia, to Persia, to India, and beyond. They dragged Tweega onto one of these boats. Now a year old and ten feet tall, Tweega was bound with more ropes than ever before.

Tall-Boy tried to stop the men, but it was no use. Tweega was on his way to far-off India, a gift from the sultan of Malindi to his friend the sultan of Bengal.

When the boat set sail, Tall-Boy ran out into the shallow, muddy sea as far as he could go, waving until his heart broke. Tweega saw none of this. He was in the hold below deck.

The hold was his new home. It was dark, it smelled, and it rocked and reeled in the lashing sea. It leaked and Tweega's hooves were constantly in seawater. Once, the sea rose in giant waves that crashed down on the boat and water splashed into the hold, carrying with it a brightly colored fish. Tweega could see it swimming round and round his legs until one day it disappeared.

Tall-Boy was replaced by a man who smelled of salt. Not once did Salt-Man whisper. He threw the food of unhulled rice and mold-covered beans at Tweega. He splashed him with seawater and scrubbed his coat with a coarse broom. Every time he saw Salt-Man, Tweega flared his nostrils and flattened his ears in anger. If only he could free his forelegs for one swift kick!

When the dhow arrived in Bengal, Salt-Man led Tweega off the boat. Weak from the voyage, Tweega stumbled. Twice he fell. Twice Salt-Man beat him. When the ambassadors from Malindi, who had also been aboard ship, saw Tweega, they began howling at Salt-Man.

"How could you starve the giraffe like this?"

"Why did you not clean him?"

"How can we present such a beast to the sultan?"

Then they beat Salt-Man with their long walking sticks and sent him away.

With good food and clean air, it did not take long for Tweega to get better. When Tweega's coat shone as it had in Africa, the ambassadors put bells around his neck and led him to the sultan's palace.

The Camel–Ox–Leopard of Bengal

ALONG THE WAY, crowds of people dressed in bright white cotton jostled to get a good look at this strange animal. Bells jingling, Tweega strode past them right up to the sultan, who beamed with delight.

Never before had the sultan seen such an animal.

"He is part camel, part ox, part leopard!" he cried, craning his neck and holding his hand on his jeweled turban to keep it from falling to the ground.

"A marvel of creation!" he shouted, and ordered Tweega taken to his personal garden.

The caretaker there was an old man, wise with animals. Old-Man fed Tweega fine food and pampered him. But Old-Man, for all his wisdom, did not sing to Tweega. Not once did he whisper.

Tweega often stood at the garden wall, looking out at the world, sniffing the air for any breeze that carried with it the smell of home. But there was none—only the uneasy scent of hungry tigers.

"Come away from that wall," Old-Man would scold. "Best you get used to this place. Here is where you will end your days."

But Old-Man couldn't have been more wrong.

The Chee-lin

At that moment, a fleet of immense ships from China was sailing into the harbor. The Chinese sought the treasures of the world, and when they saw Tweega, they could not believe their eyes. They babbled about his beauty, calling him "chee-lin."

"Since you admire this animal," the sultan said to the Chinese, "take him as my unworthy gift to your emperor."

The Chinese could hardly stifle their glee, and when they were ready to leave, the sultan ordered Old-Man to take Tweega down to the harbor.

On the way to their ships, the Chinese talked endlessly.

"This animal is the chee-lin, I tell you—a lucky sign!"

"Yes! Does he not have the body of a deer, the tail of an ox, and the hooves of a horse?"

"This is a good omen, and peace and good times are ahead for us all!"

But when the Chinese tried to get Tweega aboard, he was anything but peaceful. He reared up and kicked as never before. Old-Man was powerless. So, sailors surrounded Tweega and buried him beneath a writhing nest of ropes.

"Do not harm him!" shouted the ship's captain. "Do not hurt this gift of heaven. Take him below deck." That was the last that Tweega saw of Old-Man.

Below deck, the smell of animals filled Tweega's nostrils and he struggled even more to free himself. There were horses and pigs and sheep and squawking chickens, hundreds of them. Frightened, Tweega snorted and a deep sound came up from his throat as they tied him in his stall.

The ceiling of the stall was low. All the long journey to China, Tweega, now three years old and fourteen feet tall, kept his head bent as the ship jostled to and fro in the waves.

Make Way!

WHEN THE TREASURE SHIP docked in the Chinese capital of Nanjing, hundreds crowded the wharves, thousands more in the streets, waiting to see what wonders had been brought back from the foreign lands. And when they saw Tweega's long neck emerge from the ship, a gasp of surprise.

"What beast is that?" the people shouted.

Tweega turned to this sea of black hair and expectant faces.

"This is the long-awaited chee-lin!" cried the captain of the ship. "The chee-lin of peace and prosperity!"

The crowd cheered.

"Make way! Make way!" shouted the imperial police as Tweega was led down the street to the palace.

At the palace gate stood the emperor. While everyone bowed low, Tweega gazed at the grass-covered hills. While mandarins filled the air with words of praise for the emperor, Tweega nibbled at the banners high above their heads. When the fanfare was over, the emperor, who raised his head to no one, craned his neck to look at the chee-lin's beauty outlined against the blue Chinese sky.

Pleased in every way, he ordered Tweega taken to the imperial park, where a chattering little man greeted the animal as if he were a long-awaited guest.

"*Qílín lái le! Huān yíng! Huān yíng!* The chee-lin is here! Welcome! Welcome!"

Chattering-Man talked endlessly as he led Tweega to a park filled with trees and deer, running brooks and golden fish. He untied Tweega's ropes and said, "Go. You are free!"

But Tweega had struggled against his ropes for so long that when endless grass and trees stretched before him, he seemed unable to move. *Swat!* Chattering-Man struck Tweega on the hind leg with his stick. That was all it took, and Tweega set off in a gallop.

"Ayah!" Chattering-Man exclaimed, as he stood there laughing. "Look at him run!"

Red Clouds and Purple Mist

BUT THE GRASS AND TREES were not endless. The park was surrounded by a high wall.

Beyond the wall came noise and the musky scent of a million people. Every day Tweega went to the wall and stood for long hours, looking out.

One day, a painter came with his brushes and inks and made a portrait of Chee-lin. The smell of the black ink mixed with incense made Tweega nervous, and once—no, twice—he reared up and upset the painter's water pot.

But the painting was finished just the same, and the scholar flicked his writing brush to and fro, adding a beautiful poem about the chee-lin, saying that Tweega's coat was like red clouds and purple mist!

"It must be very lonely for you, Chee-lin," said Chattering-Man one evening while fireflies glowed. "What sadness—you will never see your kind again!"

But Chattering-Man could not have been more wrong.

The Scent of Home

DURING THAT NIGHT other ships returned from far-off Africa, arriving in Nanjing. And in the morning, as the Chinese unloaded their treasures, there came on the breeze the smell of home. Tweega, standing at his usual place, opened his nostrils and breathed it in. Then he heard a familiar snorting sound, and he turned. There at the gate was another giraffe!

Tweega went up to the new giraffe and the two rubbed their noses in each other's necks for just a moment, then went their separate ways.

This disappointed Chattering-Man, who kept saying, "I don't understand it. Why don't they like each other?"

But Tweega *did* like the newcomer, and sometimes the two would briefly entwine their long necks in friendship.

In his eighth year, when Tweega was almost twenty feet tall, another treasure ship arrived. This one brought not only another chee-lin and several lucky-deer (zebras) and camel-chickens (ostriches) but also the most fearsome scent of Africa: lions!

"Ayah, so little room," sighed Chattering-Man as he scurried to find a place for everyone. "We need a bigger park!"

And as if the emperor had heard Chattering-Man, he ordered the chee-lin taken to Peking, where a massive new capital was being built.

Fire from Heaven

HEEDING THE EMPEROR'S COMMAND, Chattering-Man herded Tweega and the other giraffes down to the river and loaded them onto barges. Up the Grand Canal the chee-lin sailed, their heads as high as pagodas.

When they arrived in Peking, workmen were scurrying everywhere, carrying stone-colored bricks and brilliant yellow tiles to the great walls and immense halls rising out of the gray dust.

As Chattering-Man led Tweega and the other chee-lin into the new city, work stopped. The men and women wiped the sweat from their brows and fell silent. These chee-lin were an omen of good fortune and prosperity, a sign that all was right in the world.

Chattering-Man thought so too. He felt proud to lead the chee-lin to their new home, and for once had nothing to say.

But whether the chee-lin were good omens or not was hard to tell, for it happened that a year later lightning struck three of the palaces and set them ablaze.

Tweega and the other animals smelled the smoke and raised their heads in fear. In the distance, they saw the flames leap up and send the yellow roof tiles bursting into the air.

It wasn't until the next afternoon, when the fire was finally out, that Chattering-Man brought hay and cabbages for Tweega. Chattering-Man shook his head and sighed, "You may be the chee-lin of good fortune, but none of us can really know what the future may bring."

For once, Chattering-Man was right.

Whispering-Girl

THE YEARS CAME AND WENT. On a day no different from the others, an old lady of high rank appeared with her servant girl.

Old-Lady sat on the viewing balcony in the park, watching Tweega and the other chee-lin, while her servant girl poured her tea and fed her sweets. The two returned the next day and the next until they came every day. On one of their visits, Chattering-Man led Tweega over to the balcony. This delighted Old-Lady, and she had Chattering-Man bring him to her every time she came.

"Touch the chee-lin for me," said Old-Lady to her servant girl a few days later. "Find out how soft his coat is."

The girl went up to Tweega and whispered, "How beautiful you look!"

Then she leaned over and touched him.

"Well?"

"His coat is as soft as a colt's, my lady."

Pleased with the answer, Old-Lady put down her teacup and closed her eyes for a moment's rest. While Old-Lady dozed, Tweega was busy sniffing the girl. He didn't much care for the smell of incense in her clothes, but there was something of great interest in her long sleeves.

"You want the apple I was saving for lunch, don't you?" whispered the girl, and she reached into her sleeve and held it out to him.

That's all it took for the girl and the giraffe to become friends—an apple and a whispering voice. Every day, Whispering-Girl would bring Tweega an apple, carefully hidden in her sleeve, and while Old-Lady napped, she'd give him the secret treat. It wasn't long before a glimpse of Whispering-Girl would bring Tweega running. Not since Tall-Boy had Tweega felt so content.

Soaring Dragons—Dancing Tigers!

TIME QUIETLY SLIPPED BY, and Tweega grew old. At twenty-six, his bones ached from the damp and the cold, and now, on this cloudy summer morning, he seemed to be more tired than usual. But what a morning to feel tired!

"Chee-lin, get up!" cried Chattering-Man as he looped a silk halter over Tweega's ears and round his muzzle. "The emperor is coming!"

But Tweega would not or could not move. Frantic, Chattering-Man sent a runner to bring Whispering-Girl. He turned to Tweega: "She'll be here soon, Old One. If anyone can put you on your feet, she can."

Whispering-Girl arrived out of breath. She called from the viewing balcony. Tweega looked up and slowly rose to his feet. And just in time—for at that moment, the emperor, the Lord of Ten Thousand Years, appeared with his teacher, his ministers, and his many servants.

"Your Majesty," said his teacher grandly, "the great chee-lin!"

The emperor's eyes opened wide with delight. What boy of nine would not be excited to see such a strange animal? The emperor ran to the railing. Startled, Tweega stepped back.

No one but Tweega noticed as Whispering-Girl reached into her sleeve. With the promise of an apple, Tweega moved forward. The boy emperor leaned over and gently touched him.

"How funny he feels!" exclaimed the boy. The loud voice startled Tweega a bit, but he never took his eyes off Whispering-Girl.

"I remember the day when this chee-lin came to the court of your great-grandfather," said his teacher.

"But where did he come from?" asked the boy.

"He was brought from India on a treasure ship, Your Majesty. And before that, they say, he came from a land far to the west."

Whispering-Girl had never heard this before, and she listened to the teacher as he told a fanciful story about the chee-lin, a story filled with so many soaring dragons and dancing tigers that it made the boy emperor laugh.

A Summer Rain

AFTER THE EMPEROR and his teacher had left with the ministers and countless servants, Whispering-Girl leaned over and gave Tweega the apple hidden in her sleeve. "What a lot you have seen, my Chee-lin! What a story *you* could tell!"

Then she turned to go, her silk clothes whispering as she hurried back to her lady.

The summer mist now came down out of the mountains and floated through the pine trees. Chattering-Man took off Tweega's halter, talking endlessly about how well everything had gone with the emperor.

Tweega turned and walked into the park. Tired after a few steps, he lay down in the grass. A light, warm rain began to fall. It danced on his coat without making a sound.

As the warm rain picked up the scent of the dry grass on the hills and the dust turning to mud on the streets of Peking, it brought back a memory of Africa. The smell drove away the fragrance of the pine trees, the cooking fires, even the incense from the yellow-tiled palaces.

Tweega, the chee-lin, opened his nostrils and breathed in the smell of home and felt at peace.

The Open Gate

There's really nothing more to tell. Tweega was old, and for a giraffe, he had lived a long life.

Some say that heaven's messengers took him home that summer's day.

Others say that he escaped from the imperial park. They mention a gate left open by a careless servant girl. But how could that be? Surely, someone would have spotted a tall-necked beast roaming the streets of Peking.

But the chee-lin, they agree, went into hiding. He'll be back one day, a sign of happiness and good fortune for all.

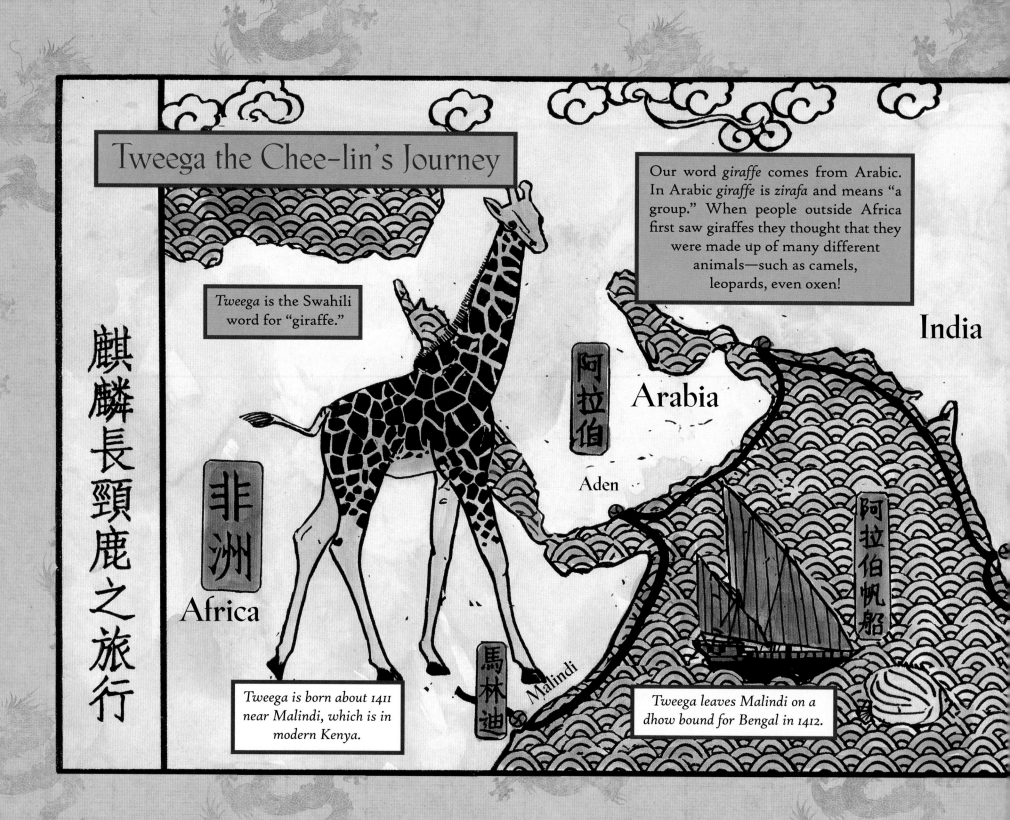

Tweega the Chee-lin's Journey

麒麟長頸鹿之旅行

Our word *giraffe* comes from Arabic. In Arabic *giraffe* is *zirafa* and means "a group." When people outside Africa first saw giraffes they thought that they were made up of many different animals—such as camels, leopards, even oxen!

Tweega is the Swahili word for "giraffe."

India

阿拉伯 Arabia

Aden

非洲 Africa

阿拉伯帆船

馬林油 Malindi

Tweega is born about 1411 near Malindi, which is in modern Kenya.

Tweega leaves Malindi on a dhow bound for Bengal in 1412.

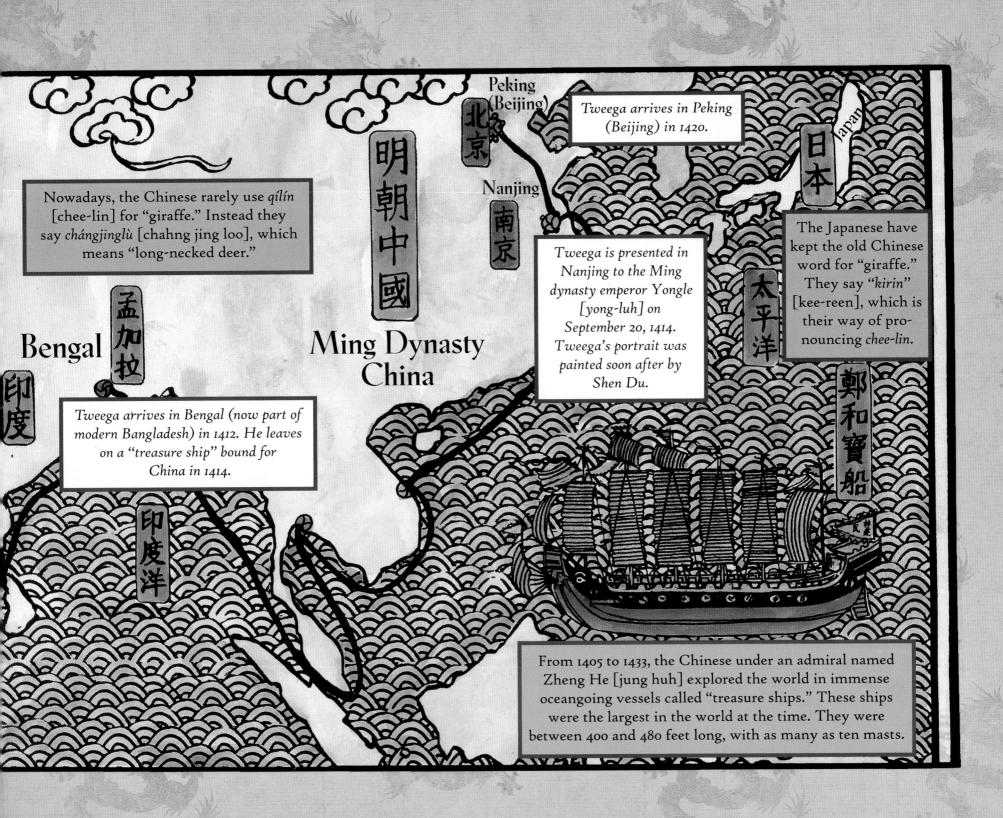

Peking
(Beijing)
北京

Nanjing
南京

明朝中國

日本 Japan

太平洋

鄭和寶船

Bengal
孟加拉

印度

Ming Dynasty
China

印度洋

Nowadays, the Chinese rarely use *qílín* [chee-lin] for "giraffe." Instead they say *chángjínglù* [chahng jing loo], which means "long-necked deer."

Tweega arrives in Peking (Beijing) in 1420.

The Japanese have kept the old Chinese word for "giraffe." They say *"kirin"* [kee-reen], which is their way of pronouncing *chee-lin*.

Tweega is presented in Nanjing to the Ming dynasty emperor Yongle [yong-luh] on September 20, 1414. Tweega's portrait was painted soon after by Shen Du.

Tweega arrives in Bengal (now part of modern Bangladesh) in 1412. He leaves on a "treasure ship" bound for China in 1414.

From 1405 to 1433, the Chinese under an admiral named Zheng He [jung huh] explored the world in immense oceangoing vessels called "treasure ships." These ships were the largest in the world at the time. They were between 400 and 480 feet long, with as many as ten masts.

西南之陬大海之滸實生麒麟身高五丈
麋身馬蹄肉角踠踠文采焜耀紅雲紫霧
趾不踐物游必擇土舒舒徐徐動循矩度
聆其和鳴音協鍾呂仁哉茲獸曠古一遇
照其神靈登於天府

THIS BOOK WAS LARGELY BASED on a painting of a giraffe done by Shen Du [shun doo] in 1414 and on the few surviving books and records of the Chinese voyages of exploration commanded by the Chinese Muslim Zheng He [jung huh]. When the imperial court withdrew its support of these voyages after 1433, much information was destroyed, making it difficult to find out what happened when China began to explore the world during the reign of Yong Le [yong luh] (1403–1425).

Two books that did survive from that period were written by men who traveled with Zheng He. These two men were Ma Huan and Fei Xin [fay shin]. They briefly mention a giraffe but say little else. No one knows who cared for Tweega or where he lived and when he died. These things are part of my story.

The boy-emperor I mention was Yong Le's great-grandson, Zheng Tong [jung tong], who came to the throne in 1436 after the short reigns of his father, Xuan De [shwan duh] (1426–1436), and grandfather Hong Xi [hong shee] (1425).

Shen Du was a calligrapher of the imperial court. His portrait survives and shows a round-faced old man with white whiskers. On the back cover, page 24, and on this page, I wrote out the Chinese text of Shen Du's poem about the chee-lin. Here is my translation:

At the edge of the great south sea far to the west,
A real cheelin was born and grew to fifty feet.
Its body: a deer's with hooves of a horse and soft, dark horns.
Its marks: a blaze of red clouds and purple mist.
It must choose its way so it tramples nothing.
Slowly, gently, it moves in harmony with all things.
Listen to its peaceful call—the sound of a chiming bell.
How tender this animal is, seen only once before.
Its spirit shines, climbing to the stars.

I painted the illustrations in this book with casein, which is a type of poster paint made with milk so that the paint will dry hard. Painting with milk has been done for a long time, some say since the days of the cavemen.

I did the backgrounds surrounding the paintings largely on the computer. The designs were inspired by African baskets and cloth, Persian tiles and Indian rugs, Chinese brocades, porcelain, and cloisonné.

www.houghtonmifflinbooks.com

The text of this book is set in Hightower and Phaistos
Book design by Carol Goldenberg

Library of Congress Cataloging-in-Publication Data
Rumford, James, 1948-
Chee-lin : a giraffe's journey /
written and illustrated by James Rumford.
p. cm.
ISBN 978-0-618-71720-0
1. Giraffe—Anecdotes. I. Title.
SF408.6.G57R86 2008
599.638—dc22
2008001863

Printed in China SCP 10 9 8 7 6 5 4 3 2 1